Oh, fish whiskers and ling lies!
Some people tell stories about mermaids and
their wild, wicked ways, but Madeline is the friendliest
mermaid you could ever meet.

~

Anna Fienberg *tells fabulous stories about fantastic and magical things. Her books for young readers include the* Tashi *series,* Minton Goes!, The Hottest Boy Who Ever Lived *and* The Amazing Tashi Activity Book.

Ann James *is one of Australia's favourite children's book illustrators. She has illustrated many award-winning picture books, including* Lucy Goosey, *by Margaret Wild,* Chester & Gil, *by Carol Faulkner, and the* Audrey of the Outback *series, by Christine Harris. Ann is also a director of the Books Illustrated Gallery.*

Madeline the Mermaid

Anna Fienberg

pictures by Ann James

ALLEN&UNWIN

Anna Fienberg would like to thank the Literature Board of the Australia Council for its assistance.

This paperback edition published in 2010
First published in 1995
First paperback edition published in 1998

Allen & Unwin
83 Alexander St
Crows Nest NSW 2065
Australia
Phone: (61 2) 8425 0100
Fax: (61 2) 9906 2218
Email: info@allenandunwin.com
Web: www.allenandunwin.com

National Library of Australia
Cataloguing-in-Publication entry:

Fienberg, Anna.
Madeline the mermaid / Anna Fienberg; illustrator, Ann James.

ISBN 978 1 74237 228 0

Mermaids – Juvenile fiction
Other Contributors: James, Ann.

A823.3

Cover and text design by Sandra Nobes
Colour reproduction by Splitting Image, Clayton, Victoria
Set in 13 pt ITC Galliard by Tou-Can Design
This book was printed in January 2010 at Everbest Printing Co Ltd
in 334 Huanshi Road South, Nansha, Guangdong, China.

10 9 8 7 6 5 4 3 2

For Madeleine, a Friday child A.F.

For two Tassie mermaids,
Sarah and Jessie A.J.

Contents

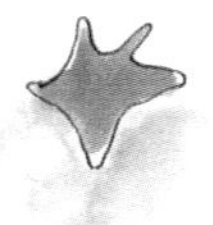

The Mermaid with Wild Yellow Hair

Madeline was a mermaid. She had a silvery tail like a fish, and shells shone in her wild yellow hair. Every day she swam and dived and ducked through the waves, and at night she headed home to the coral reefs of the sea.

Madeline lived in a conch shell with her merdog called Byron and her mercat called Bella. Bella was good with her paws. She'd made Madeline a bookcase and an attic and a carpet of coloured coral.

Madeline did somersaults with the dolphins and played hide and seek with the sardines. In the evenings, she sat on her favourite rock and sang dreamy mermaid songs. But the most surprising thing about Madeline was this: when she sang, a golden light flashed from her tail.

Like a torch, Madeline lit up the sea world around her. Dolphins basked in her light, and ordinary old bream glittered like moon slivers. All the sea creatures loved Madeline's light, and they crowded around to watch themselves glow.

Now some people told stories about mermaids and their wild, wicked ways. They said mermaids sat on rocks and sang sailors to their death.

'Beware the evil song,' they cried, 'of the terrible, beautiful mermaids!'

'Pff!' said Madeline. 'Fish whiskers and ling lies!' For Madeline was the friendliest mermaid you could ever meet.

She would have been the *happiest* mermaid, too, with her merdog called Byron and her mercat called Bella, if it hadn't been for just one thing: in the deepest bed of the ocean, on the *other* side of the world, lived the Kraken.

The Kraken was a horrible monster with tentacles as long as a whale's tail, and suckers that stuck like glue. But most dreadful of all were his eyes: two black holes that sank like wells, down, down into the pit of his skull.

Now some people also told stories about the Kraken and his wild, wicked ways. They said his tentacles could pull ships down under the waves, and that he ate sailors three in one gulp.

'Pff!' said the Kraken. 'Fish fibs and tuna tales!'

But no one heard – because no one dared to come near him. From far, far away, fish heard where the Kraken slept, and who he was eating, and where he was heading. No one wanted to be touched by those tentacles as long as a whale's tail.

Madeline, like everyone else, had heard about the Kraken. But she wasn't scared.

'He lives on the other side of the world. He could never find *me*!'

But the Kraken had heard about Madeline. He'd heard too, about mermaids and their wild, wicked ways. That didn't scare him. No, what scared him most was the dark.

Dark water and dark moving shapes and fins that blackened the sea. Things that swirled in the dark. Dimness and bubbling gloom. That's what the Kraken hated.

Ever since he'd heard of Madeline's light, he could think of nothing else. He wanted that light for himself. No longer would he have to peer into the gloom, and shake. No more would he wonder what was stirring darkly behind him.

'I'll find that mermaid and swallow her,' he said to the barnacles on his head. 'Then I'll be able to light up the dark!'

Well, the barnacles told the sardines, and the sardines told the swordfish, and the swordfish told the mercat called Bella.

'Madeline, Madeline,' miaowed Bella, 'the Kraken is coming to get you!'

Bella put bars on the conch shell and stones above the attic. Byron practised a growl that made sharks shiver.

Then Madeline and Bella sat inside, paw in hand, waiting. Byron hid behind the sofa.

With every day the Kraken crept closer. The dolphins told the bream, and the bream told the bass.

'He's just a week away,' they whispered.

'He's just a day away,' they cried.

'He'll be here in an hour!'

And the crabs scuttled off into the sand.

Inside the conch, Madeline and Bella and Byron felt the walls shake.

'He's here!' barked Byron. He growled fiercely from under the bed, but the sound of grinding stones on the roof grew louder.

'Look up there!' Bella yowled.

They saw two enormous eyes, cold and deep as wells. Then the conch rocked and roared, the walls split like eggshells, and the staircase crumpled into dust.

'Come here, Madeline, and show me your light!' bellowed the terrible voice of the Kraken.

And there he was, looming before them with his tentacles lashing and his eyes, his terrible eyes, freezing them down to their bones.

'It's time for mermagic,' whispered Madeline. And in a shaking voice she chanted:

'Come, squid, bring the dark of night,
Squirt your ink and drown the light!'

There was a swirl of currents, and through the coral reef an army of squid came rushing, squirting their inky fluid as hard as they could.

The sea grew black, as black as a moonless night.

'Let's go,' cried Madeline. 'Now, before he finds us!'

The Kraken heaved and flung about in terror. His great tentacles thrashed so hard that tidal waves rolled from China to Peru. He gave such a cry of despair that Madeline's tender heart was touched, and she stopped.

'What are you afraid of?' she asked.

'The dark,' groaned the Kraken. 'I'm afraid of the nasty, gloom-gurgly dark.'

'So, now you've seen the worst?'

'Yes,' whispered the Kraken.

'And what has happened to you?'

Silence.

'What *could* happen to you?' Madeline asked. 'You're so big, nothing in all the seas could harm you.'

The Kraken considered. He unclenched his tentacles. He stared into the dark. It seemed friendlier now, with the echo of Madeline's words.

'It's not so bad. It's not so bad at all,' he said, and he frisked a little, causing an ocean liner several kilometres away to roll.

Madeline sang two small notes and a dim light silvered her tail. As the ink cleared and she could see again, she noticed a light flicker in the Kraken's eyes. In the soft glow she could see down, down, deep into their darkness, and nestling in the centre of his eyes, like coins at the bottom of a well, was a pair of twinkling lights.

'You have stars in your eyes!' said Madeline, surprised.

'Stars?' asked the Kraken. 'Let me look.'

And he peered into Madeline's mirror.

'I can't see any stars,' he sighed. 'And aren't there stories about my terrible, horrible, black, black eyes?'

'The stories are wrong,' Madeline said firmly. 'No one has ever been close enough to see you properly before, that's all.'

Madeline opened her throat and burst into a joyful song of welcome. With the first bar, her light flashed bright, and the Kraken saw her wild yellow hair and the shells that shone in her curls.

He saw dolphins grin and bream glitter like moon slivers. He had never seen the sea world shine like this before.

'I'd like to be your friend instead of your dinner,' Madeline said softly.

The Kraken paused. He'd never had a friend before.

'We could try,' said the Kraken. 'But what about your wild, wicked ways?'

'Pff!' said Madeline. 'Jellyfish bones and sailors' skirts! I'm the friendliest mermaid you ever could meet.'

Horatio the Jellyfish

'You're a drifter at heart,' the jellyfish told her son fondly. 'Just like your dear father before you.'

'What happened to *his* father before *him*?' said young Horatio Jellyfish, who liked to set things straight.

'He tended to get stuck in seaweed, and was eaten by an eyeless violet sea snail,' said his mother. 'So let that be a warning to you, my darling: drift far but cautiously, on the great sea of life.'

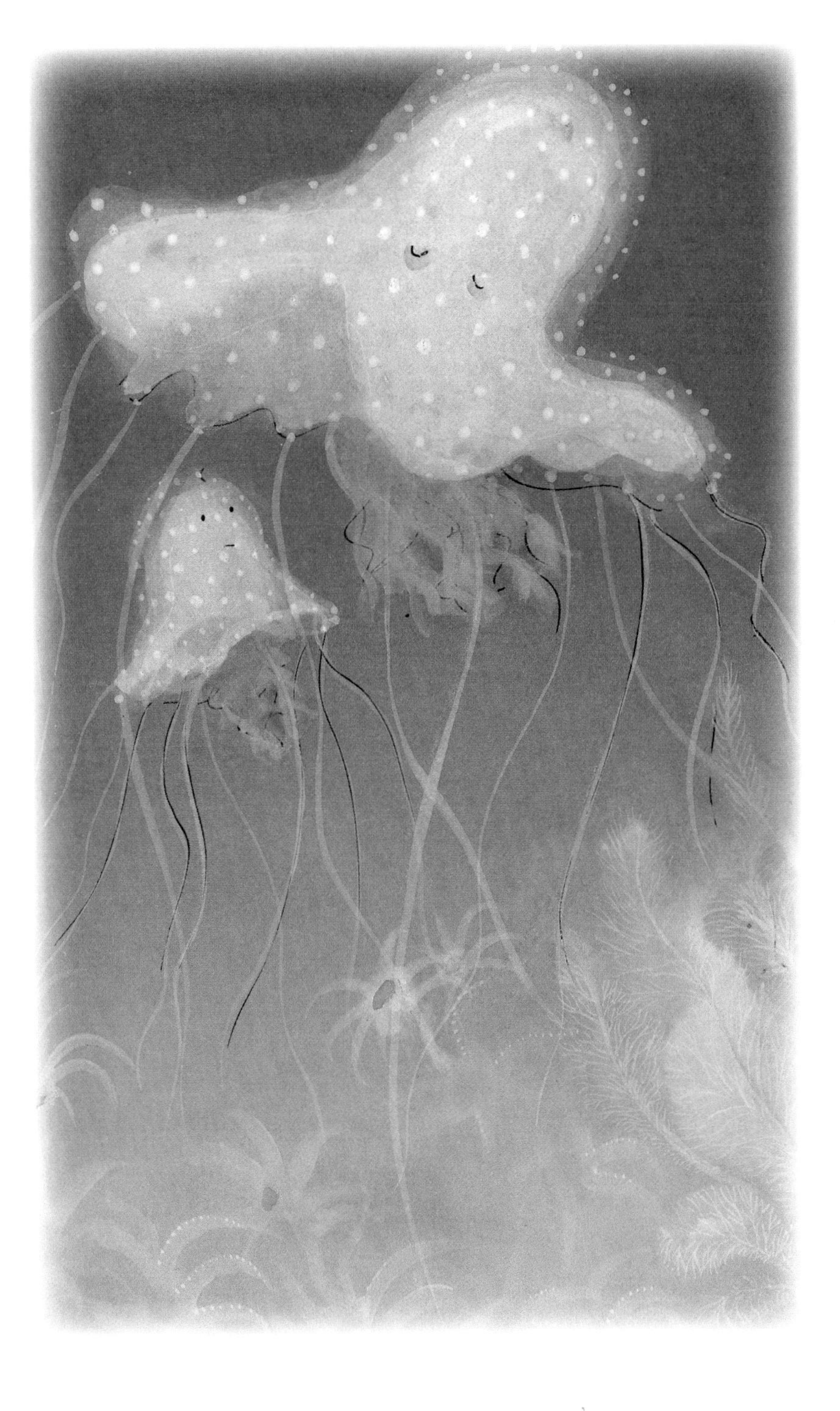

She was about to say more when a wave from the great sea of life lifted her up and away, and the two were separated for ever.

'Mamma!' called Horatio Jellyfish. 'Mamma, come back!' But only the slippery slap of the sea echoed his lonely cry.

Horatio shivered. He stared at the empty ocean, and his heart plunged to the tip of his tentacles. How could he go on drifting without his mother? She had been the only anchor in his life, the one thing he could count on. She was the one who had warned him about the deadly Pufferfish and the stinging coral, not to mention the terrible Sea Witch who kept eels in her boots. Yes, his mamma had always been there, clutching his little tentacles tightly in her own.

Horatio floated sadly on. He passed blue sea stars and angelfish the colour of the sun.

Coral shrimps called out good morning, and butterfly fish freckled the waves. But Horatio saw nothing.

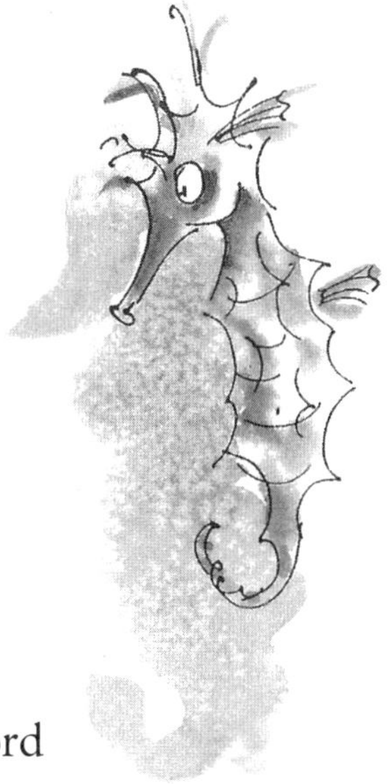

Only the memory of his mother trembled before his eyes.

Horatio drifted like this for twenty-three days. Occasionally he would have a word with a sea urchin or fill in a minute or two with a fairy basslet, but as soon as the conversation grew interesting, the current would tug him, and away he floated.

That was the trouble with being a wanderer, thought Horatio Jellyfish. You may travel and see the world, but you could lose your mother, and you never had a conversation lasting more than a wavelength. You could never hang around long enough to make a friend.

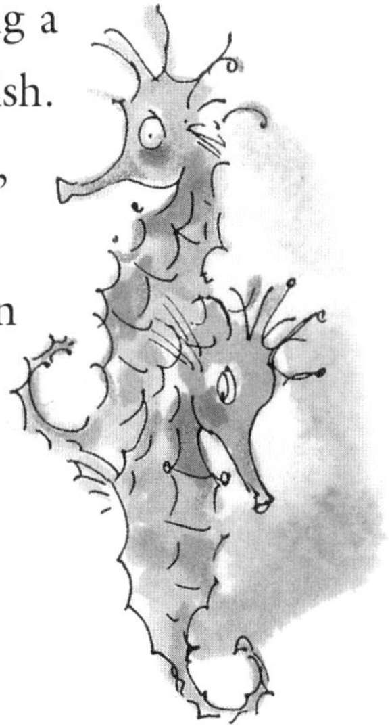

'I may be a drifter at heart,' he told a banana fish as he passed by, 'just like my father before me, but what I'd really like is to have a good rest on a rock and a decent chin-wag with someone.'

Horatio was drifting past a forest of red coral when something unusual caught his eye. Down below he saw a golden light shining. It lit up the water so that he could see cuttlefish changing colour for dinner, and sea-horses swapping their news.

On all his travels, Horatio had never seen anything as beautiful as this light. The current pushed him along, closer and closer, until he was floating right up to the centre of the light. It streamed from the window of a large conch shell, and now he could hear an enchanting song coming from inside.

A mermaid with wild yellow hair opened the door and saw Horatio drifting by. Suddenly he was bathed in golden light so that his tentacles shone like Christmas ribbon. Madeline the mermaid nodded in her friendly way, but continued to sing as if her life depended on it.

'Hello, my friend,' she sang in F major, 'pardon me if I sing so loudly, but my voice is my only defence.'

'Defence?' asked Horatio. 'Defence against what…or whom?'

How could the owner of such a magnificent, miraculous, melodious voice ever have an enemy?

But just then the great sea of life heaved again and Horatio drifted helplessly away.

'*Always* interrupted!' he exploded. 'Never hear *anything* to the end.' And he shook his tentacles in disgust at the waves.

It was two whole days before he passed

the conch shell again, and heard the voice once more.

Madeline opened the door and nodded in her friendly way. But her voice was weak, and the light glowing from her tail was trembling.

'Hello, Horatio,' she sang in D minor, and she glanced anxiously at the house of black coral beside her. A rumbling noise was coming from there, strangely like someone talking at a hundred kilometres an hour.

'Is that your enemy?' asked Horatio.

'Ye-e-es,' sang Madeline. 'My friend the Kraken usually lives there. We are neighbours now. But the Kraken went to visit his sister who has fallen tragically in love with a merman, and has lost the will to live. How I wish he were here now,' and her voice deepened an octave, 'instead of that poisonous pest.'

'Who is it?' whispered Horatio.

'The Pufferfish!' cried Madeline.

Horatio gasped. He had heard stories about the Pufferfish, the most boring fish in all the sea. The Pufferfish was famous for talking endlessly, using long and difficult words to describe things like the mating habits of the terebellid worm or what his Great Aunty Platter had eaten for breakfast the day before yesterday. As he talked, he puffed up to twice his size with words and importance and deadening ideas. Personally, Horatio wouldn't have minded meeting the Pufferfish. No discussion could last too long for him. Still, others had gone cross-eyed and died of boredom after just two minutes of pufferfish conversation. He was an extremely dangerous creature.

'I'm singing so that I can't hear his dreaded words,' sang Madeline.

'And I'm practising my meditation,' said Bella the mercat. 'Om, om, om,' she purred her mantra loudly.

'But we can't go on being noisy for ever,' barked Bella's friend, Byron. 'We haven't eaten or slept for days, and still old Pufferfish is droning on.'

And in the heartbeat of silence, they all heard him.

'... and really, Madeline, it is most peculiarly opportune that I discovered the Kraken's residence to be without inhabitants. There will be multifarious opportunities for me to tell you about the manifold branches of my family. I know you are *avid* to hear all about them. My second cousin Tiberius, for instance. Tiberius is *the* great authority on herma – Madeline, where are you?'

At that moment, when everyone began singing and talking loudly again, the current pushed Horatio along, nearer and nearer to the house of the Pufferfish.

'Scream!' sang Madeline.

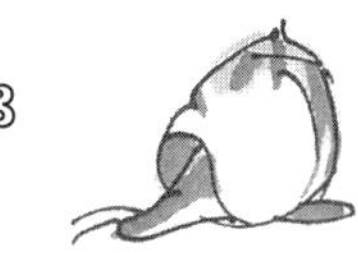

'Say your two-times table!' wailed Bella.

'What comes after ABC?' barked Byron.

But Horatio kept silent. As the door of the black coral house opened and a beaked nose shot out, Horatio suddenly knew that his life was about to change for ever.

'Oh, now I see you, Madeline,' said the Pufferfish. 'As I was saying, cousin Tiberius knows all there is to know about the hermaphroditism of the fairy basslet fish.'

'Excuse me,' said Horatio. 'But what is hermaf – what you said?'

'Hermaphroditism,' answered the Pufferfish, 'as I was just about to elucidate to our young gelatinous friend, is that condition in which an animal is both male and female – at one and the same time.'

Horatio was thinking. On his many travels he had actually met a school of fairy basslet, and he had noticed that they had some very strange habits.

'Pardon me,' he said, 'but I think what happens is that sometimes the female turns into the male.'

'Pardon *me*,' exclaimed the Pufferfish, 'I am perfectly cognisant of that fact.' He turned to Madeline. 'I was just about to divulge the fascinating details of this curious phenomenon to you when this mucilaginous person interjected.'

'Oh, sorry,' Horatio gulped.

The Pufferfish began to breathe heavily, and with every breath he grew larger. In a flash he had doubled his size. Now he looked very dangerous indeed.

Just then the current changed again and Horatio began to drift away.

'Act precipitately,' called the Pufferfish, 'and inosculate your tentacle around my beak. I wish to continue this line of argument, as one is so seldom acquainted with a jellyfish of such exceptional manners and informed mind.'

Horatio wanted to keep chatting, too, but he looked warily at Madeline and her friends.

Madeline nodded encouragement, and he saw the glint in her eye.

Without losing another second, he shot out a tentacle and latched onto the hard surface of the Puffer's beak. He skidded to a stop. Then he whipped the tentacle around it another ten times.

'Nsosh sho shtightshly!' gasped the Pufferfish.

'What?'

'Undosh shor shtentaclesh!'

'Not until you give us all your promise,' cried Madeline.

She grinned joyfully around her, at her beloved Byron and Bella (who had stopped saying 'om') and at last at the brave and clever Horatio.

'What golden silence!' she said, and closed her eyes for just a moment.
Then she opened them and glared at the Pufferfish. 'Promise us, you puffed-up old wind-bag, that you will no longer bore anyone to death.'

'Shno!' breathed the Pufferfish.

'Tighten your tentacle, Horatio!' cried Madeline.

Horatio did so, but he said 'Excuse me' under his breath.

'*Now* will you promise, you great garrulous gas-bag? Otherwise Horatio here will keep your beak closed for ever!'

'Shawlrighth, shawlrighth, shi promish!' And suddenly the Pufferfish was free as Horatio loosened his tentacle and smiled.

'That is the first time I've stayed in one place for more than a wavelength – it was heaven!' Horatio said. 'Could I wind a tentacle harmlessly around your tail and hang here for a while? We could talk about your Great Aunt Platter or fairy basslets or whatever you like.'

The Pufferfish looked at Madeline.

'You can talk to Horatio,' said Madeline, 'but if I hear that you have bored him or anyone else, watch out! Because you know what happens when a promise to a mermaid is broken.'

The Pufferfish did know, but that's another story. *This* story ends happily ever after, with Horatio having a long, long chin-wag (with no interruptions) and a good rest.

And if he stays in one place long enough, even his mamma is sure to drift by.

The Sea Harpy

On a tropical island, in the middle of the southern seas, there lived a handsome pirate captain. Every day was a party for Captain Plunder because he was rich from ten long years of looting. He had a band of twenty-five steel guitars, a diamond tie-pin as big as a golf ball, and a darling pet python named Patrizia. If you'd seen him lounging against his palm tree, reading *The Tropical News*, you'd have thought he was the luckiest pirate in the southern seas.

But deep in his heart, Captain Plunder nursed a secret sorrow.

Now at the bottom of the southern seas, below the tropical island, there lived an awesome sea harpy called Tsss. Nobody ever went near her, but everyone had heard of the sinister snakes that grew from her head. 'Tsss! Tsss!' the snakes hissed, and their bite had more venom than a stonefish spire.

Tsss had the body of a fish, but she had a human face and scaly arms, and her talons were razor sharp.

No one knew the sea harpy's real name, and no one knew about her secret love.

But most mornings, Tsss swam up from the bottom of the sea and bobbed about near the shore of the island. She looked longingly at Captain Plunder, admiring his curly red beard and black tattoos. But Captain Plunder never saw her, because he was too busy picking the chocolate almonds from his teeth, and thinking about his secret sorrow. From where he sat, Tsss looked like a barnacled bit of flotsam and jetsam.

'Oh, Plunder, my dear,' Tsss would whisper, 'when will you see the real me?'

At night she would swim back home, back to the sunken shipwreck where she lived with the bones of ten drowned sailors.

It was dark and silent down there, with just the clink of the sailors' skeletons knocking against the wood. There she would wait until dawn, thinking of past days and weaving her schemes for future happiness.

Meanwhile, in the conch shell with the carpet of coloured coral, Madeline the mermaid was preparing to meet a Human Friend. She combed her wild yellow hair and clipped pearls on her ears.

'What a waste – all for a creature without a tail,' sighed Bella the mercat.

Madeline smiled and sprayed 'Seaweed Passion' on the nape of her neck.

Once a year Madeline had to find a Human Friend, and stay with him for a day, or the human half of her would fade and the fishy part would take over.

This year Madeline had spied a handsome pirate on a tropical island. She liked his curly red beard and black tattoos, and decided that he would make an excellent Friend.

Madeline polished her nails, picked up her bag and kissed Bella goodbye. She was just a speck in the distance when Bella remembered the hat.

'Your hat!' cried Bella. 'You forgot your hat!' But Madeline had disappeared behind a wave.

'I thought she looked fine as she was,' said Byron, as they gazed into the distance.

'Oh, you know about as much magic as a sea snail!' sniffed Bella. 'Don't your realise that without her magic hat, Madeline's meeting won't last five minutes? Her Friend will drown.'

Bella sped up into the attic to fetch the hat, but when she opened the chest, it was empty.

Bella wrung her paws. 'Someone has stolen it,' she growled softly. 'There'll be a drowning before the day's end, you'll see, and our dear Madeline will become just another fish in the sea.'

Byron hurried to her side and stared thoughtfully at the chest. 'Who could have taken it?' he wondered. They answered together – 'Tsss! Let's go!'

Madeline, meanwhile, was looking into the eyes of Captain Plunder. She was singing a romantic song, and the golden light from her tail dazzled the angelfish in her wake.

'Handsome pirate with the big black tattoos,
Munching chocolate and reading The News,
Oh, how I need you to be my Friend,
Just for a day and then it must end.'

Captain Plunder rubbed his eyes and stared at the vision below him. He leant out a bit further over the side of his yacht. 'A real live mermaid,' he whistled, 'and prettier than a sailor's dream.'

'Dive down and join me, sailor most bold,
And I'll tell you tales from days of old.'

'Oh, I love a good story,' cried Captain Plunder and he looked deeply into Madeline's eyes. They flashed and glittered like twin sapphires as she sang.

Captain Plunder leant out even further, until his hand was trailing in the water. Just then, near the stern, there was a loud splash, but when Captain Plunder turned round he saw only a barnacled bit of flotsam and jetsam bobbing in the sea.

Madeline held her slim white arms up over the waves.

'My magic is strong but I'd never use force,
Come hear my sweet songs, 'fore I grow too hoarse!'

The pirate couldn't resist her singing a moment longer. With a strangled scream he dived off his yacht and into the sea.

Madeline gave a smile of welcome and reached into her bag for the magic hat.

'Help!' gasped the captain. 'How could I have forgotten? I never did learn to swim!'

Frantically Madeline turned her bag inside out. Captain Plunder thrashed about in the sea like a groper caught in a net. Madeline tried to hold his head above water, but Plunder knew his end was near.

'It's a real shame,' he told Madeline. 'I still had lots to do, places to see. I've never even been to Monte Carlo. And who will look after Patrizia? Please give her all my chocolate almonds.' And he sank below a wave.

Suddenly the barnacled bit of sea rubbish near the stern sped towards Madeline and the disappearing Captain Plunder. When Madeline heard the 'Tsss! Tsss!' of coiling serpents, she shivered right down to her fish tail.

Tsss flung her arm out of the water, holding up the magic hat. 'Tsss! Tsss!' the snakes spat, and she caught the captain by his ear. Holding the hat high in the air she said, 'If you wear this hat you'll be saved, my darling, but only if you promise to forget this treacherous mermaid, and marry *me*! Tsss! Tsss!'

Captain Plunder eyed the snakes writhing around the harpy's head and he opened his mouth to say, 'Never!' but he swallowed a great gulp of water instead.

'I promise,' he spluttered. But his face was green and he flinched at the sight of her talons.

And so Tsss placed the magic hat on the captain's head and he sank down under the waves with her, his hand in her scaly claws. Down they swam, and down further still, until they reached the shipwreck and the bones of the ten dead men.

'My ship! My crew!' cried Captain Plunder, looking around, and his tears melted into the sea. 'I was the only one saved that dreadful day the ship went down. The waves were roaring and the wind was screaming and the ship ran onto a reef. I watched the woman I was to marry disappear for ever into the storm.'

'How much did you love her, tsss! tsss?' asked the sea harpy.

'I loved her more than my life. I wanted to die with her, but I was washed ashore. And now,' he sobbed, 'in place of my beloved I'm to marry a harpy with serpents on her head and barnacles on her skin.'

The snakes lunged at the captain and he swung round to see Madeline swimming up behind him. She put her finger to her lips and mouthed, 'Trust me.' Then she placed her hand on the hat and sang three low notes. The ten skeletons stirred and sat up.

'Come on, my friends,' cried Madeline, 'all together now, grab the sea harpy by her serpents, they can't harm your old bones, and wrap her up in this sail.'

The ten skulls grinned in the murky light. They flicked aside darting tongues and needle fangs, and bundled Tsss up in the old sail. When it was done she lay neatly rolled, her sea-serpent hair tied together on her head like a bunch of deadly flowers.

'Now I want you to take her to the island and tie her to the sea wall at the entrance to the bay,' said Madeline. The skeletons nodded and picked up the wriggling bundle.

'I'll go, too, and show them the way,' said Byron, who had just arrived and was very relieved to have missed all the action.

And so Madeline took the captain's hand and led him home to the conch shell with the carpet of coloured coral. There Bella made a delicious lunch of smoked oysters and chocolate almonds, and they told each other stories and secrets of the sea until the following dawn.

When he returned to the island the next morning the captain gave a shout of joy. There, waiting on the sea wall, was his loyal pet python. And there beside her, tied to a ring in the sea wall, was a beautiful, dark-eyed woman.

Byron swam up to join them. 'You'll never guess,' he barked. 'As soon as the sun rose, the old harpy began to fade away like dew in the sun. Her scales dropped off, and that's all that's left of those snakes.' He pointed to a pile of mouldy skins that lay at the woman's feet.

'Patrizia?' whispered the captain.

'Plunder!' murmured the woman.

When the captain had undone her ropes and embraced his dear, secret sorrow, she told him of the spell that the jealous Sea Witch of the West had put on her, the dreadful day of the storm.

'Only if you promised to marry me, ugly as I was, and bring me back here, would her spell be broken. Well, you didn't give your promise gladly, but then I must admit Tsss was a fearsome sight, and I never really cared for sea snakes myself. Now, Plunder my dear, I think we should be married straight away and – what do retired pirates do?'

'They sail the Seven Seas one more time and make a stop at Monte Carlo. Then they buy a nice little tropical island and settle down.'

'Just what I had in mind,' agreed Patrizia.

The captain bent to give her the first of the 1,256,000 kisses that were to bless the rest of their lives.

'There's just one more thing I would like to ask,' Patrizia interrupted him. 'Could we please change the name of your python?'

And so they did.

The Sea Witch War

Madeline was reading a book called *Adventure Stories for Mermaids* when she looked up at her window to see the Pufferfish, and attached to him by a long tentacle was her dear friend Horatio Jellyfish.

'Hello, Madeline,' said Horatio, floating up towards her.

'Salutations and greetings,' said the Pufferfish. 'We have converged upon your good home to tell you –'

Horatio gave him a warning nudge with his tentacle. 'The stonefish are sick, Madeline,' he interrupted. 'Hundreds of them are dying along the west coast of the island. The spikes on their backs have turned as soft as seaweed –'

'As flabby and flocculent as noodles,' added the Pufferfish. 'As droopy and doughy as dandelions –'

'And so they just creep along the floor of the ocean, eating nothing, and growing skinny,' finished Horatio.

'How strange,' said Madeline. 'I must go there and see.'

But as it happened, later that day Madeline's friend the Kraken arrived back from a long and tragic voyage, so Madeline forgot about the stonefish for a while.

At dinner that night, when the Kraken had finished his 5,267,314th mussel, he said, 'Something strange seems to be happening on the western coast of the island.'

‘Oh, fish whiskers and ling lies!’ exclaimed Madeline. ‘I forgot – the stonefish are sick.’

‘Are they?’ said the Kraken. ‘Well, I don’t wonder. What *I* noticed was that the coral is turning white. Red, blue, black, yellow – all the forests of coral have gone as white as snow. It’s eerie.’

‘Curiouser and curiouser,’ murmured Madeline. She was wondering if the sick stonefish had anything to do with the strange case of the colourless coral, when Bella the mercat swam in, bursting with more strange news.

‘Someone has taken the salt from the western seas!’ she cried. ‘The fish are dying – they’re foaming white about the gills. It’s horrible!’

Madeline frowned. 'Now this has gone too far,' she declared as she gave Bella a pawful of shrimps.

'What has?' barked Byron.

'There's magic at work on the western coast,' said Madeline darkly. 'And there's only one creature powerful enough to weave such spells.'

'The Sea Witch of the West!' cried Bella. And Byron buried his nose in his paws.

The following dawn, Madeline put her mirror and comb in her bag and set off for the western coast. She swam for a day and a night, until she reached the rocky shores of the coast. The water was thick with spells, and Madeline had to swish her tail hard and mutter her magic to keep herself moving.

She threaded her way through the ghostly coral and surfed the waves to come ashore.

'Mighty Hinnykins, Sea Witch of the West, come and speak with me,' she cried.

And there, popping out from a small castle in the sand, came a tiny creature no bigger than Madeline's thumb. She was dressed in seaweed, and she kept little eels in the heels of her boots. She had one fish eye and a smile as crooked as a bend in a river. She was tiny, but her magic was bigger than all the water in the western seas.

'What do you want, Mermaid?' crackled the witch. 'I'm busy.'

'So I see,' said Madeline. 'Was it you who softened the stonefish spines, took the colour from the coral, and robbed the sea of its salt?'

'Of course it was me,' said the witch proudly. 'Did you think that great clumsy Sea Witch of the East could dream up such interesting spells as those?'

'Ah!' exclaimed Madeline. 'So you two witches are having another contest?'

'A war of magic, young fish tail,' the witch snorted. 'And it's only just beginning. I'll empty the ocean if I have to, and *then* she'll know who is the greater witch!'

'You'd end the world just to prove your power,' muttered Madeline. 'But think, if there's nothing left for you to magick, what then? Who will feel your power?'

The sea witch spat into the sand, but her human eye widened.

'Listen, I have an idea,' Madeline said quickly. 'This contest of magic needs a judge – someone who can see the truth of your great power. There'll be no favours – no friends or foe. Only the power of true magic will win.'

'And who do you suggest will be the judge?'

'The great monster Kraken and I could be your judges. We will each set you a task, and whoever best performs the tasks will win.'

'I have no fear of your tasks,' the witch said. 'But the Sea Witch of the East will tremble.'

'We'll see,' said Madeline. She picked up her mirror and gazed into it. And as she gazed, her own reflection faded, and a new face appeared. The eyes were small and black but the mouth was as big as a cave. It opened and four rows of teeth glowed greenly, slimy with algae.

'Who summons the mighty Lobloma, Sea Witch of the East?' the face said.

Madeline told her, and described her plan for the contest.

'I have no fear of your tasks,' said the witch. 'But the Sea Witch of the West will tremble.'

And so Madeline took her mirror and comb and swam for a day and a night until she reached the conch shell where her friends were waiting.

'In two days the sea witches will come,' Madeline told them. 'I must choose a task for them.'

Madeline still found time to read another chapter of her book before she had to meet the witches. It was about an adventurous merman with green eyes and a cheeky smile. Madeline sighed as she read.

Hinnykins, the Sea Witch of the West, was the first to arrive. She paddled a tiny canoe made from a palm leaf, and her two little shark's-tooth oars went whooshing through the water, quick as the wind, as she sped towards the rock where Madeline and the Kraken sat waiting.

'Has that big lump of lard arrived yet?' she asked.

'Are you talking about me, you little dust-crumb?' boomed a voice behind her.

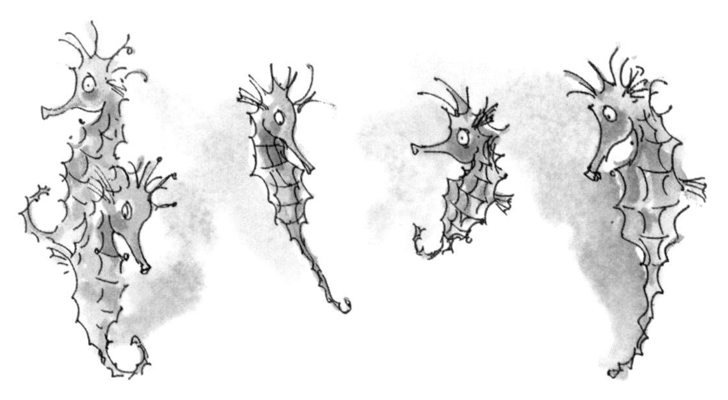

Lobloma, the Sea Witch of the East, sat astride a chariot of shells, drawn by an army of sea-horses. She was really no taller than Madeline, but she was as round as a melon, and cushions of flesh bulged over the great gold rings she wore on her fingers.

'Now that you're both here,' began Madeline, 'I will set the first task.'

'The worst of luck to you, you pinch of grit under the nails,' spat Lobloma of the East.

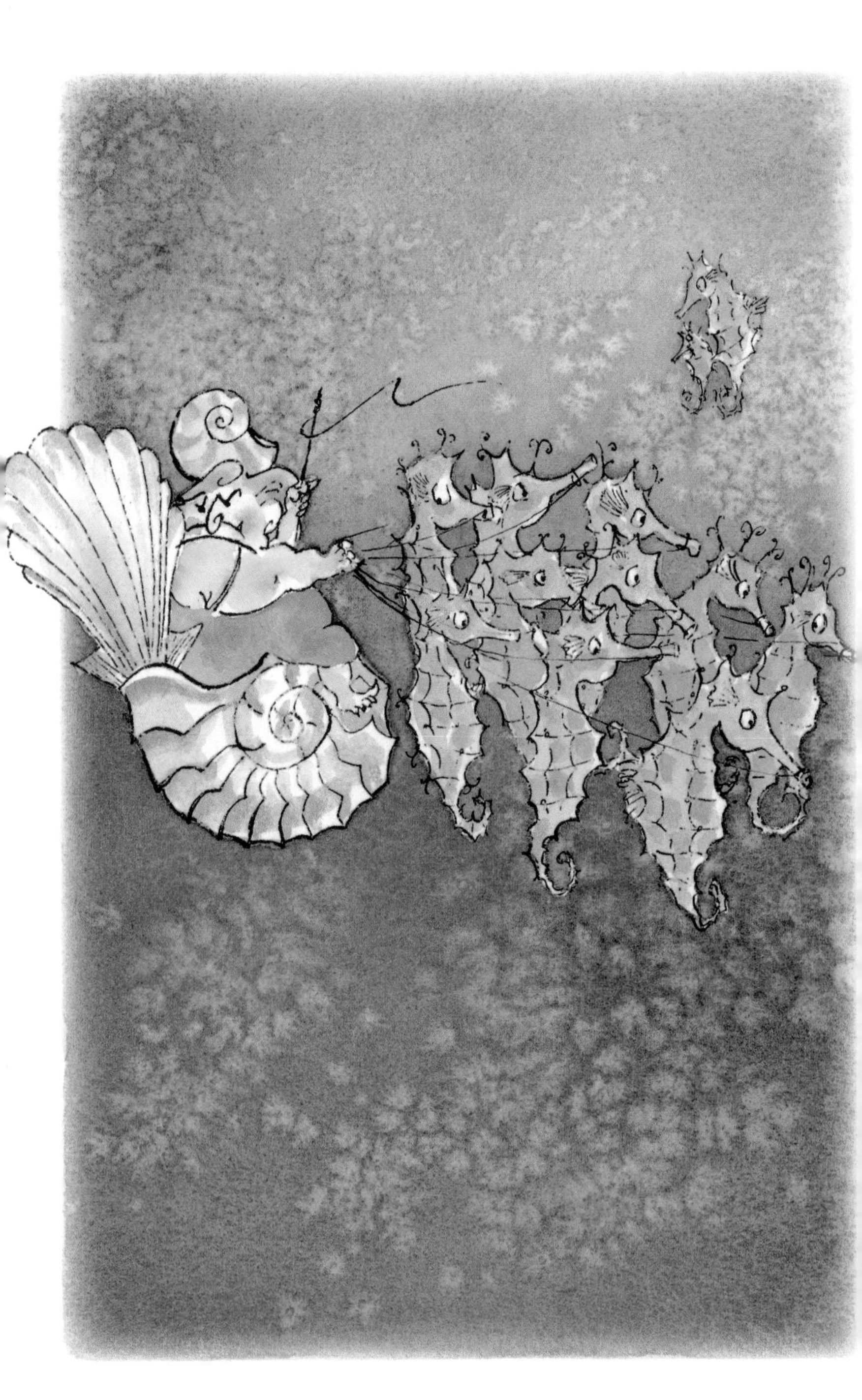

'The evil eye to you, you lily-livered lubber loaf!' replied Hinnykins of the West.

'For the first task,' Madeline cut in quickly, 'you must both discover my heart's desire and bring it to me.'

There was silence for a moment as the two witches looked long and deeply at Madeline.

'For the second task,' the Kraken made his voice crack like thunder, 'you must both discover *my* heart's strongest desire and bring it to *me*.'

And once again the witches were silent as they stared into the dark wells of the Kraken's eyes.

'You couldn't bring anything larger than a prawn head, you gob of nose ooze,' sneered Lobloma.

'That's enough, now begin!' bellowed the Kraken, and both witches, muttering under their breath, set off in opposite directions.

Tales of the witches' doings spread all around the ocean. Horatio Jellyfish saw the small witch talking to gulls and listening to whispers of the sea grasses. A handsome pirate captain was questioned by the large witch until his ears burned and his wife pleaded, 'Mercy!' As the days passed, the waves throbbed with magic, with the witches weaving their spells and searching the sea.

Neither Madeline nor the Kraken spoke of it, but each was secretly wondering if they would ever see their heart's desire.

The moon was full when the witches finally returned to the rock. Their hands were empty and only the small canoe and weary sea-horses bobbed beneath them. Kraken the monster and Madeline the mermaid were waiting there, but no one said a word as the stars came out and the moon rose higher and the bream leapt silver from the sea.

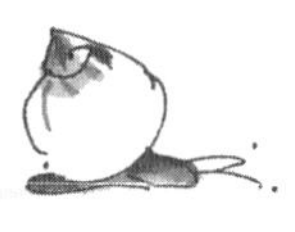

'Well, I'll be the first, Madeline, to give you your heart's desire,' said the tiny Sea Witch of the West. She clapped her hands and a dazzling rainbow-coloured mountain rose out of the sea. Madeline blinked and looked closer. The mountain was made up of sparkling polished jewels. Pearls and rubies, sapphires and diamonds, roses of silver and rings of gold.

'The world's treasure, that's what mermaids want most,' said the little witch proudly.

The jewels glowed in the moonlight, sending up a bonfire of light.

Then Madeline sighed. It was only a small sigh, but it told the witches everything they wanted to know.

'What *more* could you possibly need?' exploded the Sea Witch of the West.

'This.' Lobloma pulled off her rings and clicked them together. Suddenly, beside her, there appeared a merman. He had a human face and body, and a golden fish's tail. His face was so beautiful but unexpectedly familiar that Madeline cried out.

'A merman for the mermaid,' said the Sea Witch of the East, and she cackled with delight. For Madeline's face told her everything she wanted to know.

The merman had green eyes and brown skin that gleamed and sparkled with the silvery water. Madeline looked into his face and felt that she had known him always. She took his hand in hers and said, 'You are my heart's desire.'

'And you are mine.' The merman smiled, and kissed her.

There was a great flapping of fins as the fish swooped up over the waves and the Kraken held out a tentacle to shake the merman's hand.

'Cut the cackle!' cried the tiny Hinnykins. 'Now it's time for the Kraken's task. Only I know what lies in his heart.'

'I should go first, you little toe-nail clipping,' boomed Lobloma. 'I won the last task.'

'This isn't Monopoly, you great greedy toad!'

But the Sea Witch of the East clicked her rings again and suddenly, sprouting from her hand, was a bunch of electric eels.

They lit up the night like torches, their heads wriggling and writhing, sending arrows of light across the sea.

'That is magnificent,' said the Kraken softly, 'and months ago this light would have been my heart's desire.'

Lobloma of the East started to crow but the Kraken cut her short.

'But now I am no longer scared of the dark, and I have no need of eels and their light.'

Lobloma dropped the eels back into the water with disgust and immediately they became as small as lizards. Little Hinnykins fished them out and pushed them down into the heels of her boots.

'Now it is *my* turn,' she said, and she drew two small circles in the air. She held out her arms and slowly the air was filled with crying – the puzzled, frightened crying of a baby. Curled up on the great grey tentacles of the Kraken lay a newborn baby Kraken.

The Kraken looked down into the baby's face and stroked its smooth cheeks. His eyes filled with tears as he rocked the baby gently.

'You are the last of the Krakens, and my heart's desire,' he told it softly.

And the baby smiled.

The night was quiet now but full and soft with all the new feelings, as the mermaid and the merman held hands, and the Kraken cuddled his new family.

'This is all very fine, but where does it leave us?' Hinnykins cut in. 'We've both won a task, so now there is a draw. You two, with your stupid hearts' desires, haven't solved anything. What do you say, Lobloma?' She turned to her enemy. 'Shall we begin again? I can blind the bream and crumble the coral. Can *you*?'

'Just a moment!' Madeline rushed in. '*Any* witch could do that. But can you fly on your broomsticks to Sirius, the brightest star in the southern sky? Whoever arrives there first will be the winner, and the Sea Witch of All the World.'

The two witches were silent.

Little Hinnykins spat into the sand and tickled the eels in her boots. 'Sirius is very far,' she said doubtfully.

'Scared, are you?' sneered Lobloma. 'I'm not surprised. How could a puny piece of fish bait like you ever reach a star?'

'Your poor old broomstick would sink under *you*, snake breath.'

The Sea Witch of the East tossed her head and clicked her rings. 'The last one there is a maggot dropping!' And she magicked her broom out of the air and leapt on. Soon she was just a moving stain on the moonlit sky.

'You'll be the one who's dropping, slime gums!' the little Sea Witch of the West shouted after her. And she shot off on her broom like a fire-cracker.

'They'll still by flying and arguing this time next century,' smiled Madeline. 'Good riddance!'

Clasping hands, the mermaid and the merman dived off the rock and swam home to the conch shell where they lived happily with Bella the mercat and Byron the merdog. And in the years to come when the baby Kraken grew old enough for school, Madeline taught him all the songs she knew about the wild and wonderful ways of the sea.